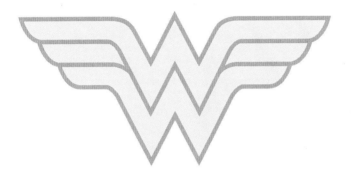

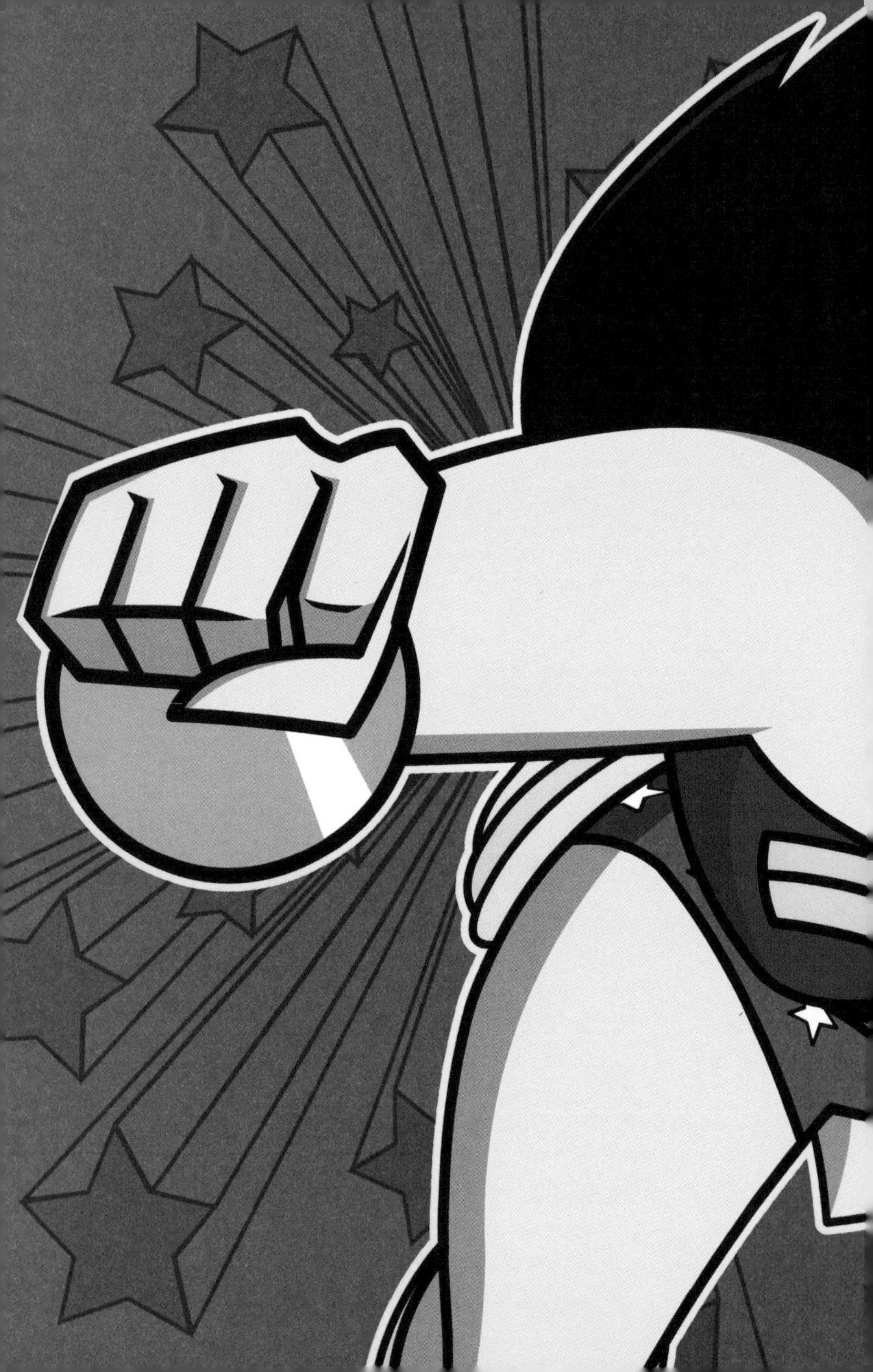

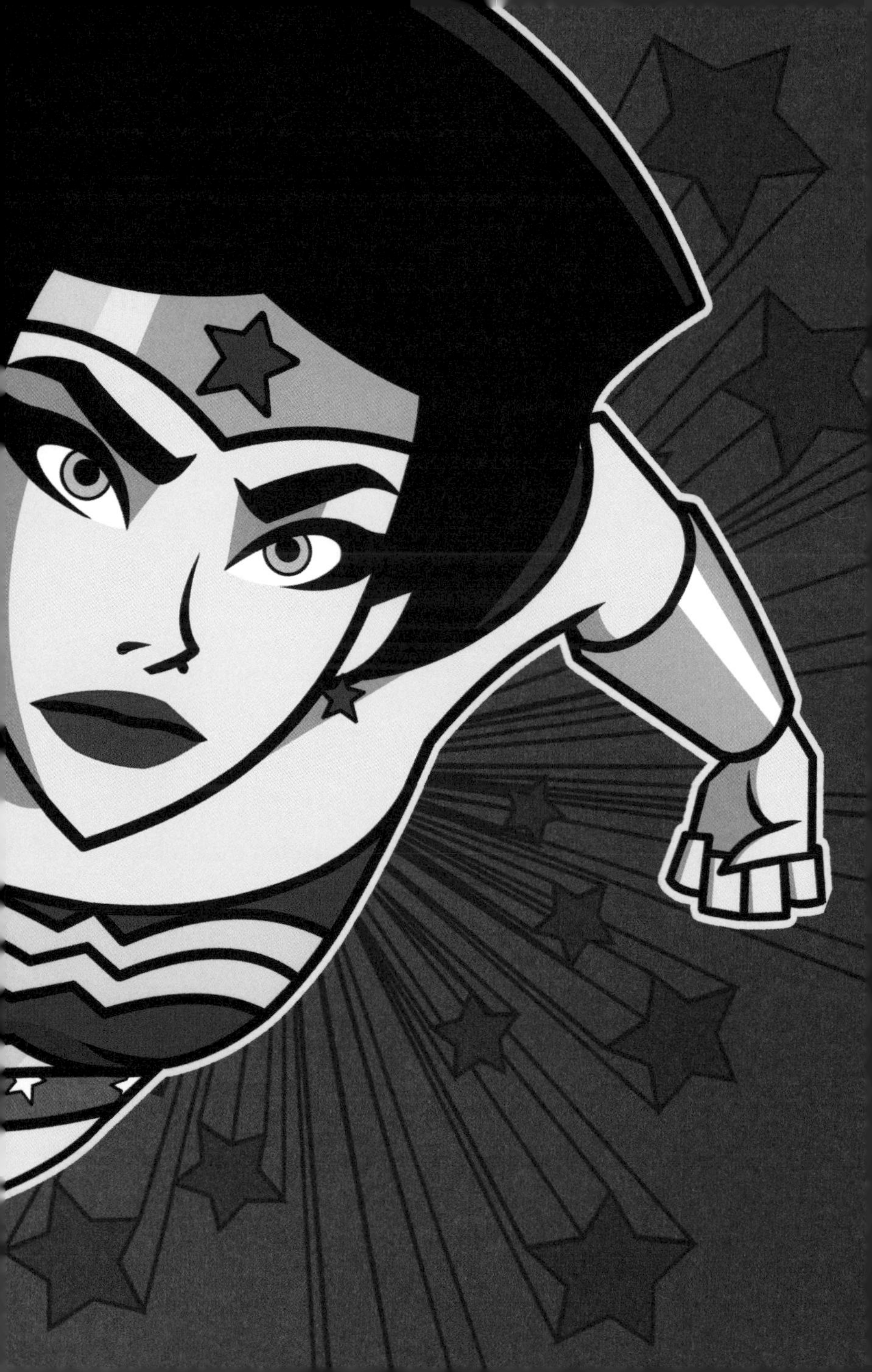

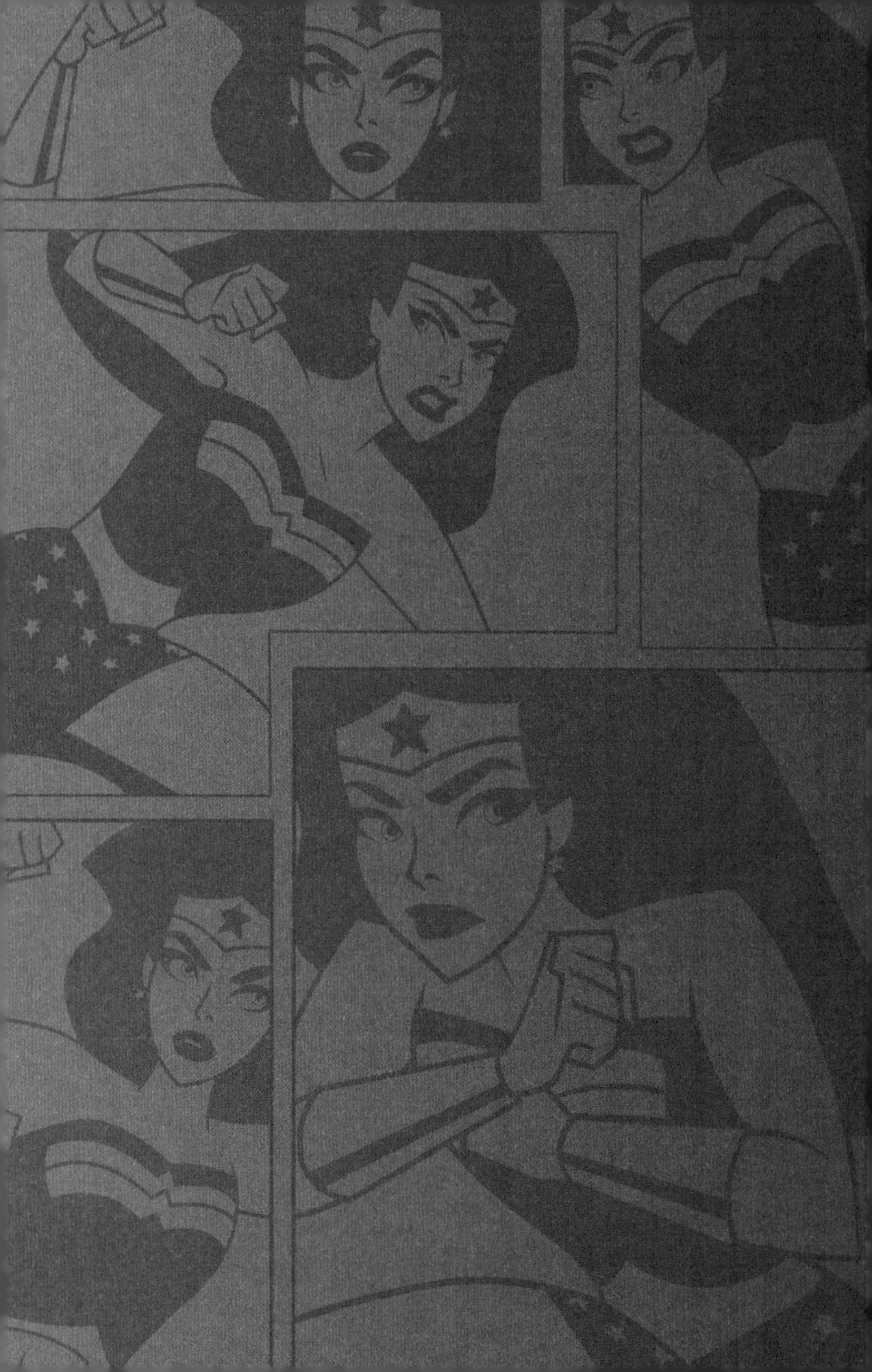

DC COMICS™ SUPER HEROES

# WONDER WOMAN™

## CREATURE OF CHAOS

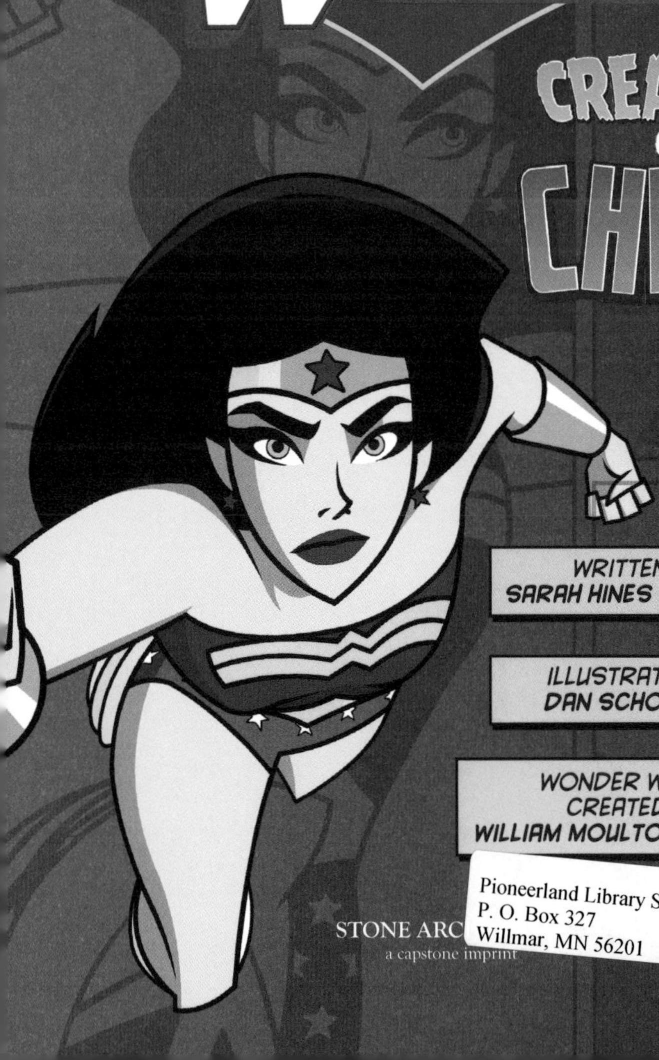

WRITTEN BY
SARAH HINES STEPHENS

ILLUSTRATED BY
DAN SCHOENING

WONDER WOMAN
CREATED BY
WILLIAM MOULTON MARSTON

STONE ARCH BOOKS
a capstone imprint

Published by Stone Arch Books
A Capstone Imprint
1710 Roe Crest Drive
North Mankato, Minnesota 56003
*www.capstonepub.com*

Library of Congress Cataloging-in-Publication Data

Hines-Stephens, Sarah.
  Creature of chaos / by Sarah Hines Stephens ; illustrated by Dan Schoening.
    p. cm. -- (DC super heroes. Wonder Woman)
  ISBN 978-1-4342-1885-8 (library binding) -- ISBN 978-1-4342-2256-5 (pbk.)
  [1. Superheroes--Fiction. 2. Pride and vanity--Fiction.]  I. Schoening, Dan ill.
II. Title.
  PZ7.H574Cr 2010
  [Fic]--dc22                              2009029098

Summary: When riots erupt in downtown Washington, D.C., only one
person can stop them . . . Wonder Woman! But as she attempts to calm the
crazy crowd, the super hero is suddenly caught off guard by an even bigger
problem. Devastation, the mind-controlling super-villain, is out to destroy
Wonder Woman once and for all. If the Amazonian Princess is going to stop
this Creature of Chaos, she'll have to face her greatest weakness . . . and learn
from the lessons of her past.

Art Director: Bob Lentz
Designer: Emily Harris

Printed in the United States of America in Stevens Point, Wisconsin.
022014   008034

# TABLE OF CONTENTS

# CHAPTER 1

# SIGNS OF DEVASTATION

The setting sun cast a rosy glow over the city of Washington, D.C. But all was not well on the streets below. Diana knew something was wrong when she heard the shouting. She felt a chill run up her spine. Somewhere in the city a fight was breaking out.

Diana was ready for her real work to begin. The only thing missing was the right outfit. **WHOODOOSH!** Like a cyclone, Diana began to spin. She became a blur of red, black, gold, and blue.

Her movements were faster than the eye could track. When she twirled to a stop, Princess Diana had vanished. In her place, Wonder Woman had appeared!

Dressed in her warrior garb, Wonder Woman looked every inch the Amazon princess she was. She was always ready to carry out her mission of peace. Since her arrival from Themyscira, the Amazons' hidden island paradise, Wonder Woman had settled hundreds of human problems.

It was not hard for her. She had love and compassion for all living things. Those were two of the most important laws in the Amazon code. She also had reason. These three things were usually enough to help humans get along peacefully. When they weren't, Wonder Woman would then be forced to use her amazing strength.

She was also armed with powerful weapons. They were gifts from her mother, Hippolyta, the queen of Themyscira. A Golden Lasso forced humans to tell the truth once they were wrapped in its coils. Shining bracelets could repel bullets and arrows. Her crown-like tiara could fly through the air and slice through metal, or even concrete. These Amazonian treasures were almost always enough to tip the scales in her favor.

She moved at top speed toward the angry voices. The shouts grew louder as Wonder Woman closed in. CRUNCH! Breaking glass added to the many noises. The uneasiness Wonder Woman felt was growing as she ran. Something told her this was no ordinary disturbance.

Then, she stopped dead in her tracks.

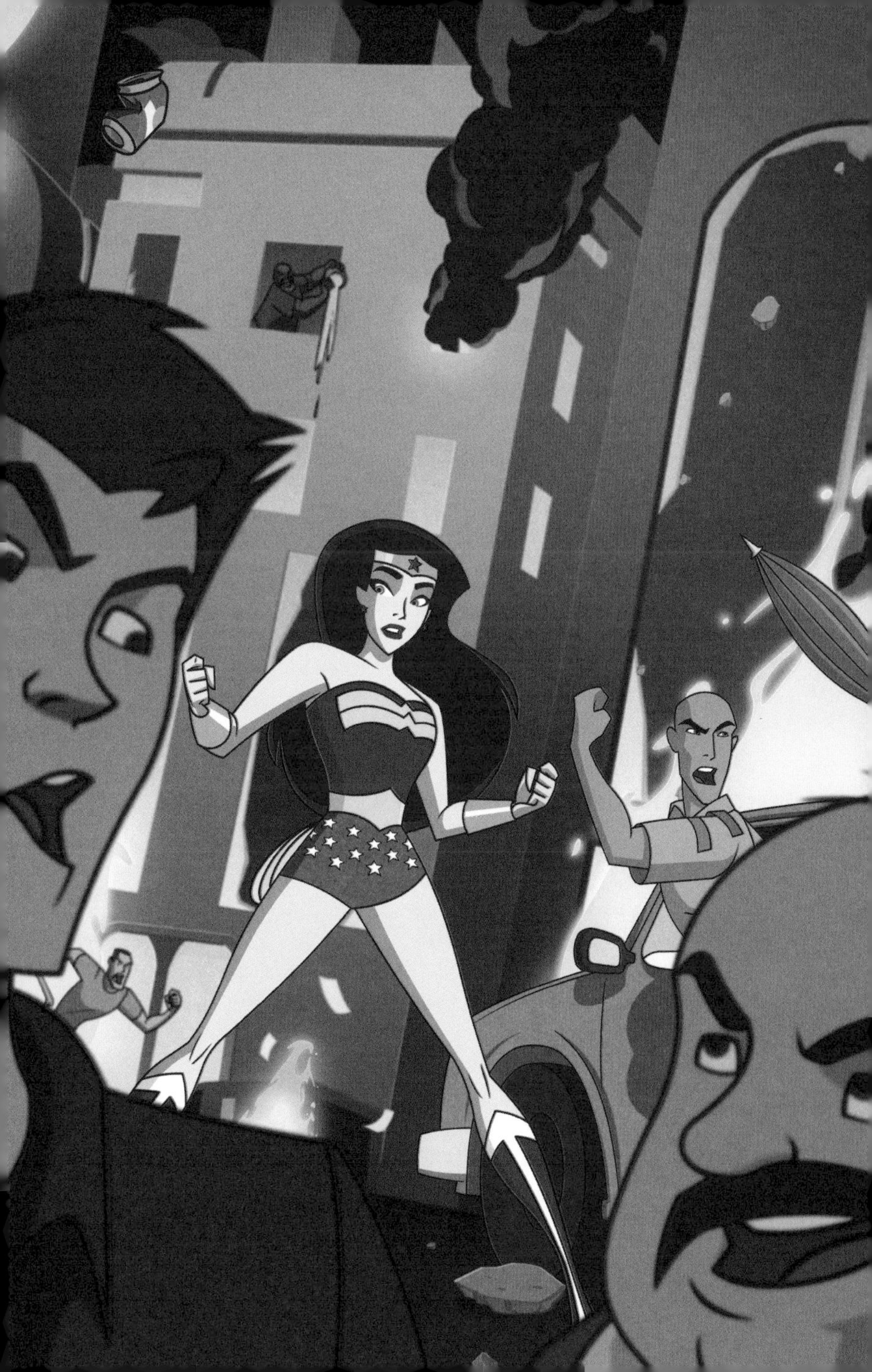

She had seen her fair share of senseless violence, but nothing compared to this. Everywhere she looked, people were fighting with each other.

Outside Bentley's Bakery, four men pounded on one another with their fists. Two doors down, groups of children ducked behind stairs to throw rocks and insults. A pair of teens yanked each other's hair and screamed like cats.

In the crosswalk, an angry woman was attacking a car that was in her way. The woman pounded the windshield with her umbrella. **SMASH!** She struck the glass until it cracked, which sent pieces flying everywhere.

Several feet away, a father and child stopped arguing long enough to protect their faces from the glass pieces.

"I'll take that," Wonder Woman said. Calmly, she pulled the metal-tipped umbrella from the woman's hand. The woman looked stunned as Wonder Woman opened the black dome. She held it over their heads.

Wonder Woman had acted just in time. Several objects struck the umbrella's fabric and bounced off. A shower of dishes rained down. Glasses and plates shattered around them.

"Hey, that could have hit me!" the woman said, ducking away from Wonder Woman. She pumped her fist at the person throwing things from a window overhead.

"You're welcome," Wonder Woman mumbled.

Usually the people she saved were grateful. But not this time. The old woman had gone back to yelling and swinging her purse. The little girl nearby was too busy kicking her father's ankle to notice Wonder Woman. Everyone on the block seemed blinded by rage.

Wonder Woman quickly realized something. She could probably get the people to stop fighting long enough to talk to them. But there was no way they would be able to see reason.

Taking great strides, Wonder Woman walked deeper into the heart of the chaos. She knew there was more to the mess than her eyes could see. She needed to find the source of these strange events. Along her way, Wonder Woman disarmed more brawling citizens.

Jutting out a powerful arm, Wonder Woman grasped a bat. She yanked it from a thug's hands before he could pound his victim. With the quick swipe of her heel, she toppled another attacker. He fell flat on his back. **THUD!**

Her efforts were not enough. A moment later, the attacker was back on his feet and swinging his fists. Wonder Woman needed to find the real culprit quickly.

Just then, she spotted the source of the chaos. A young girl was sitting on top of a smashed car. Her hair was red and wrapped in barbed wire. Her black suit and purple cape set off her pale skin and icy eyes. Her smile was cruel and full of mischief.

Wonder Woman knew that child.

She was Devastation.

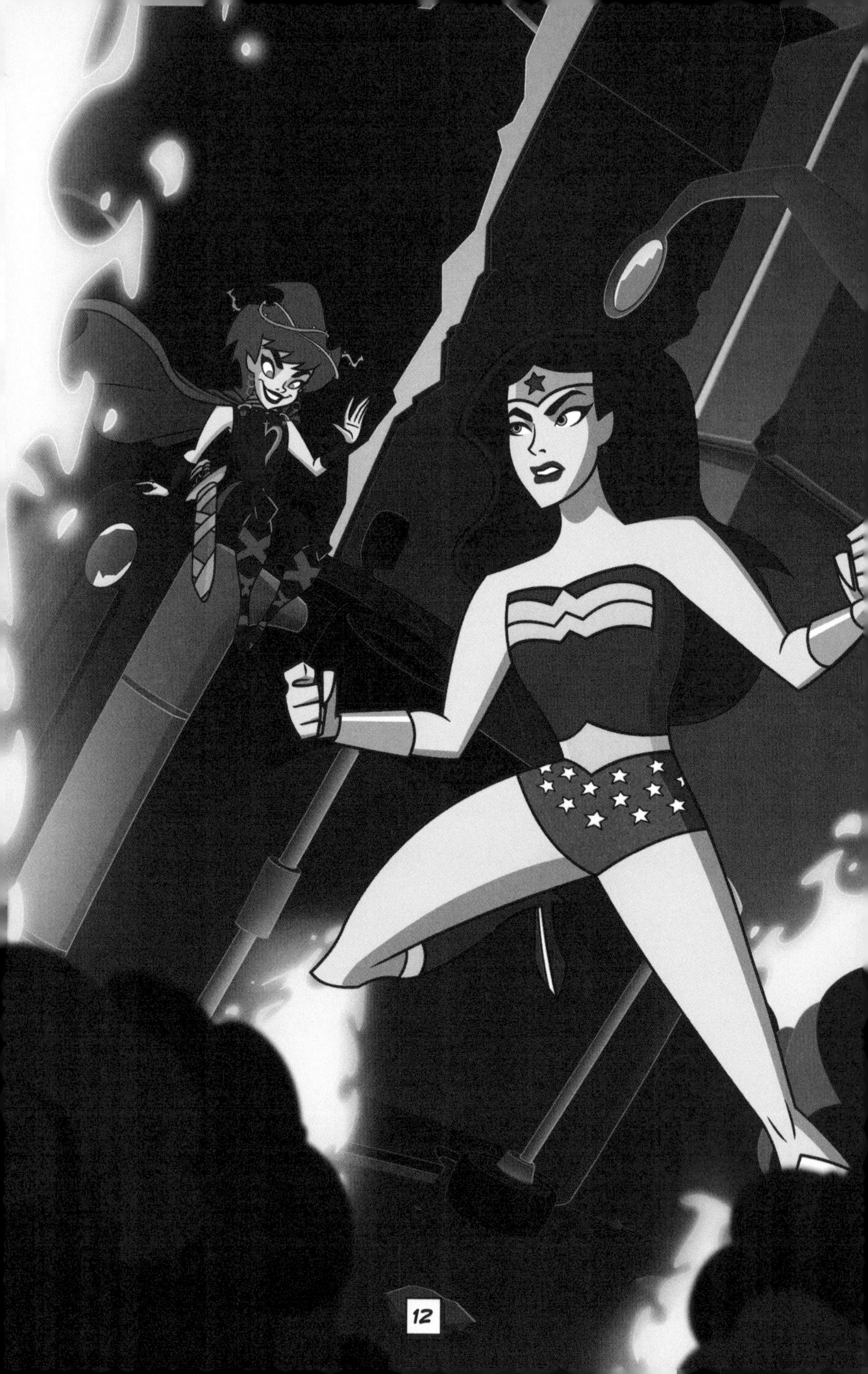

# CHAPTER 2

# DEVA

Devastation looked at the fighting in the streets and giggled. Nothing made her happier than spreading misery. After all, it was the reason she'd been created.

"Deva," Wonder Woman greeted her foe. If the baby-faced villain had been a normal child, she would have been easy to overpower. But this was no average kid. This was Wonder Woman's worst enemy.

Years earlier, when Princess Diana was born, she'd been blessed by the gods and goddesses of Olympus.

The Olympians had given her amazing wisdom, beauty, strength, and speed. She also received the ability to fly. And she could open people's hearts to peace.

But not everyone wanted to get the message.

Cronus, the gods' sworn enemy, hated baby Diana and everything she stood for. He formed a child of his own — Wonder Woman's evil equal, Devastation. Cronus then asked each of his older children to grant their new sister a gift. Speed, flight, strength, and a quick mind were all given to Deva. She also received the knowledge of how to kill any living thing. Worst of all, she could influence people's minds.

Wonder Woman spread peace and understanding. Deva spread hatred and violence.

Defeating Deva was going to be much harder than a simple babysitting job.

Deva nodded at Wonder Woman. She smiled through clenched teeth. "Princess," she hissed. Her tone was teasing. After she spoke, she burst out laughing.

Wonder Woman watched the girl closely. Deva's eyes twitched away from hers and quickly back. She was planning something.

**KRAK!** Wonder Woman turned to deflect a flying hubcap spinning toward her. The metal clattered to the ground.

Behind her, Deva laughed. This time the reason was more obvious. The fighting crowd from earlier had gathered into an angry mob. The mass of angry people was moving toward Wonder Woman.

They shouted angry threats. They hurled everything they could find in Wonder Woman's direction. They pushed forward.

Leaping clear, Wonder Woman flew up several stories. Then she paused on the ledge of a building to consider her next move.

Deva didn't wait. She jumped into the center of the crowd. She began stirring up the mob with angry encouragement.

Wonder Woman did not blame the citizens of Washington, D.C. She knew the people around Devastation could not help themselves. Their minds were being controlled by Deva's powers. Somehow she needed to separate them from Deva.

Slowly, Wonder Woman reached for her Golden Lasso.

*If I can manage to snare that troublesome teen,* Wonder Woman thought, *I could pull her away from the mob.*

Deva saw what Wonder Woman had in mind. She screamed, "That's what you think!" Her voice was surprisingly loud, coming from such a small body. Her strength and fury was surprising as well.

Deva leaped over the heads of crowd. Then she landed on the roof of a delivery truck. She pulled out her sword and pointed it at a city bus. The passengers stared, horrified, out the windows. The fear in their eyes made it clear. Somehow they had managed to escape Deva's evil influence.

With a flick of her wrist, Deva directed her mad followers toward the new target. They surrounded the bus, pushing at it from both sides. SLAM! SLAM!

The huge vehicle rocked back and forth. They were going to tip it over! Wonder Woman had to do something.

"This is between us, Deva. Leave them out of it," she demanded.

"Make me!" Deva howled back at her. **WHOOOOSH!** Wonder Woman flew straight toward the street. She landed hard. Then she raced along the ground. As she zipped beneath the bus, she was so close to the pavement that she could feel the heat coming off it.

With both arms extended, she picked up the heavy vehicle and everyone inside. She lifted it upward. **THWOOOOMMMMMM!!**

Gracefully, she soared through the air with the bus held above her. She would set the bus on the roof to keep the people safe.

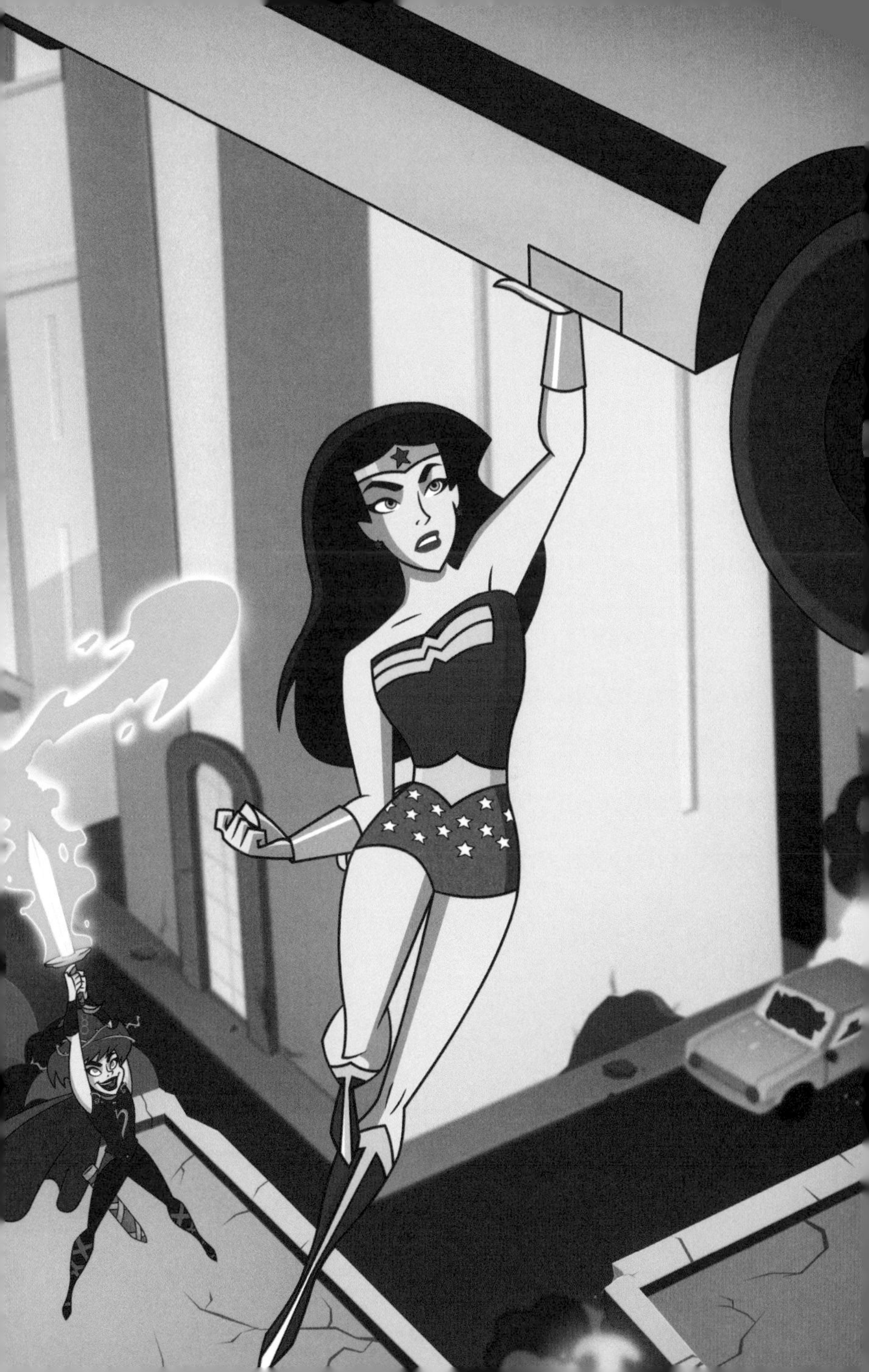

Wonder Woman was almost to the rooftop when a wave of pain roared through her. *BZZT!* It started below her ribs. Then it quickly spread through her whole body.

Wonder Woman's strength left her. She plummeted toward the ground, along with the bus — and all of the passengers inside!

The ground rushed up to meet them. Wonder Woman struggled to catch the bus and fly again, but she could not. Nothing could stop her fall. Deva had zapped the hero with an energy bolt from her sword. And the nasty brat was getting ready to do it again!

With a mighty effort, Wonder Woman pushed through the pain. It took all of her strength, but somehow she managed to stop the bus from smashing to the ground.

The mighty Amazon absorbed the full impact herself. **WHAM!** The force pounded her into the street. A huge crater opened up below the bus. Wonder Woman lay at the bottom. She was barely moving.

As the dust cleared, a little hand pushed the bus away. Deva peered into the depths.

"Why can't you play nice?" Wonder Woman said, struggling to speak normally.

"I don't like to play nice," Deva whined. "Anyway, it's time for you to go home. Isn't that your mommy calling?" Deva pointed her sword at the hole.

Wonder Woman's head swirled with pain. She could not move. She would not live through another blast.

Slowly, the edges of her vision grew darker and darker.

Struggling to stay awake, she focused on a flower growing in the cracks of the crumpled pavement.

Her world went black as she slipped into a dream of her childhood.

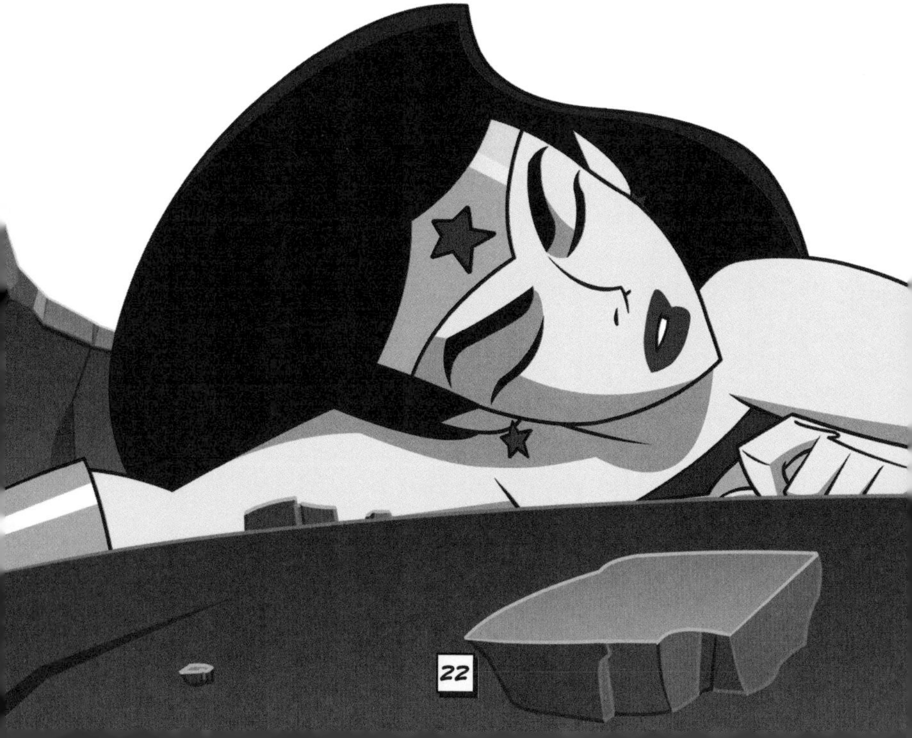

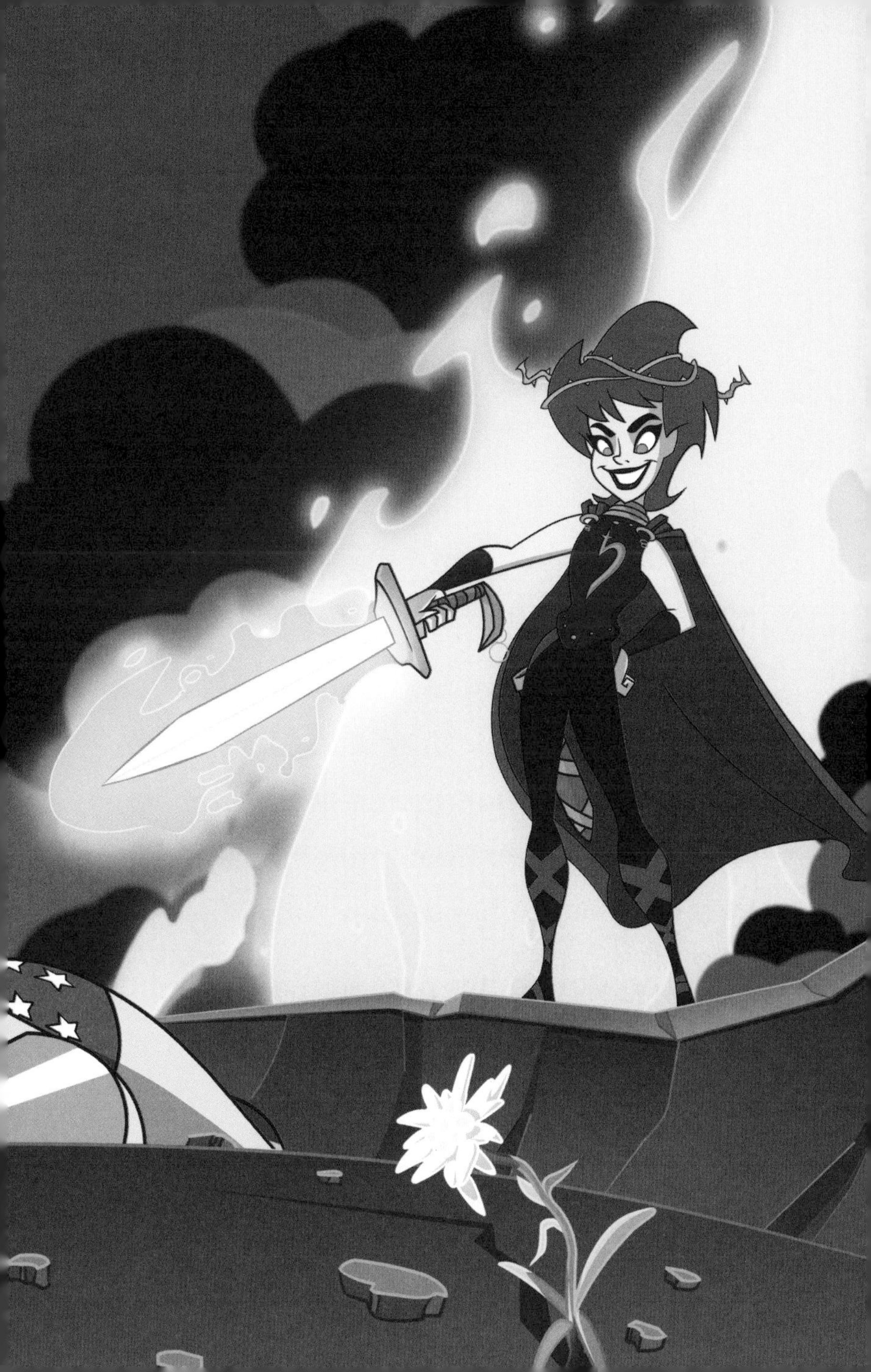

# CHAPTER 3

# CHILDHOOD MEMORIES

Diana dashed down the forest path. The wind whistled in her ears.

"Hurry up, slowpokes," she called to her trailing friends. The deer did not answer in words, but the young princess heard them anyway. They were not far behind, and they cried out to her as they ran.

Diana slowed her pace so the flock could catch up. She leaped over an enormous fallen log, and then stopped. Her eyes opened wide. She had paused to take in the beauty all around her.

Of all the wonderful places to play on Themyscira, the forest was her favorite.

The island paradise she called home had wonderful beaches, temples, lakes, and mountains. Diana enjoyed them all, but the enchanted forest held special promise. She never knew what kind of treasures she would find there. She might spy a family of rabbits in an earthen hollow, or stumble upon a whirlpool. Or she might discover a flower she had never noticed before — like the one she saw today.

"It's a good thing I stopped," Diana said to herself. "These flowers are beautiful."

Diana crouched down to get a better look at the patch of white blooms in the shadows. They were growing underneath the log. Diana could have easily missed them.

Diana imagined handing her mother a bunch of the pretty blossoms. She imagined the smile it would bring to Queen Hippolyta's face. She stretched out her arm to gather a bouquet, but the flowers were out of reach. Without thinking, Diana lifted the log that blocked her way. With only one arm, the small girl held the huge tree aloft. With the other, she gathered the blooms.

"There," she said when she had a handful. She let the huge log fall. **THUD!** Birds scattered. The forest stirred. Diana looked up. She saw Phillipus, the Amazon general who looked after her, standing in the clearing. Phillipus was in charge of Diana's safety when her mother could not be with her. The general never smiled.

"Look," said Diana, holding the flowers. But it wasn't a bouquet anymore.

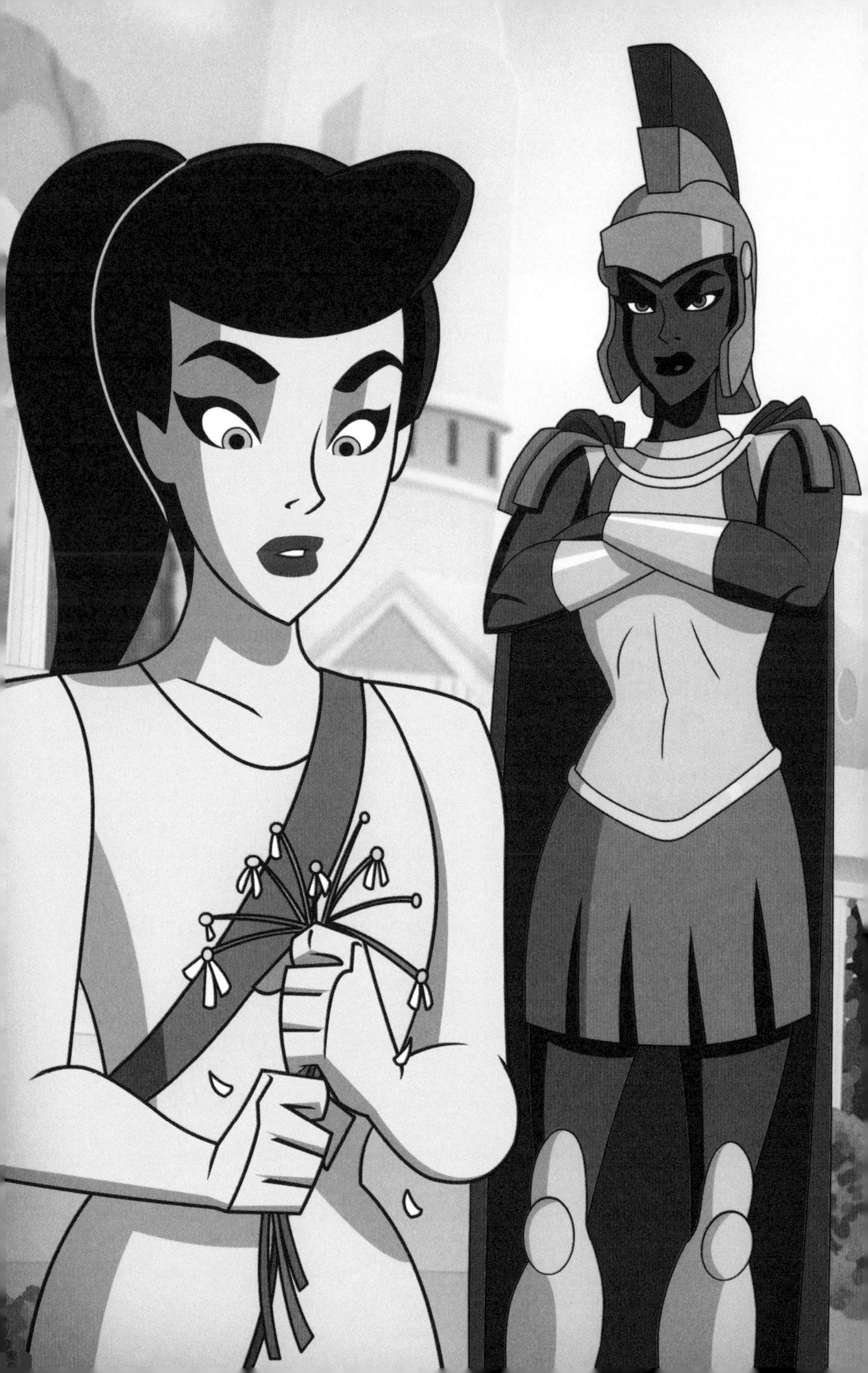

The little princess was so strong that the tender flowers had been crushed in her mighty grasp.

The crease in the general's brow deepened as she looked at the mashed mess. "You don't know the strength you possess," she said.

"I didn't mean to squish them," Diana said sadly. She'd only wanted to bring a smile to her mother's face — and maybe even the general's.

"Of course you didn't. That is the problem," Phillipus said. She was pacing back and forth. The deer, who had finally caught up, stayed hidden on the edge of the forest. Phillipus came to an abrupt halt. "With great strength comes great responsibility," she announced. "The time has come for you to begin your training."

Queen Hippolyta was not happy to hear that Diana's playtime was coming to an end. After all, she had waited hundreds of years for the gods to grant her a child. She had formed the child herself from the clay of Themyscira. The gods had then blessed and breathed life into the tiny princess. Diana was the only Amazon child ever born on the island. She was an answer to the queen's prayers. Hippolyta was in no hurry for her only daughter to grow up.

Diana, on the other hand, welcomed the training. She loved it and quickly mastered each new skill. She awoke every day at dawn. Then she thanked the gods for the gifts that helped her to excel, and she set out with Phillipus. She trained alongside her sister Amazons, learning archery, mental focus, and hand-to-hand combat.

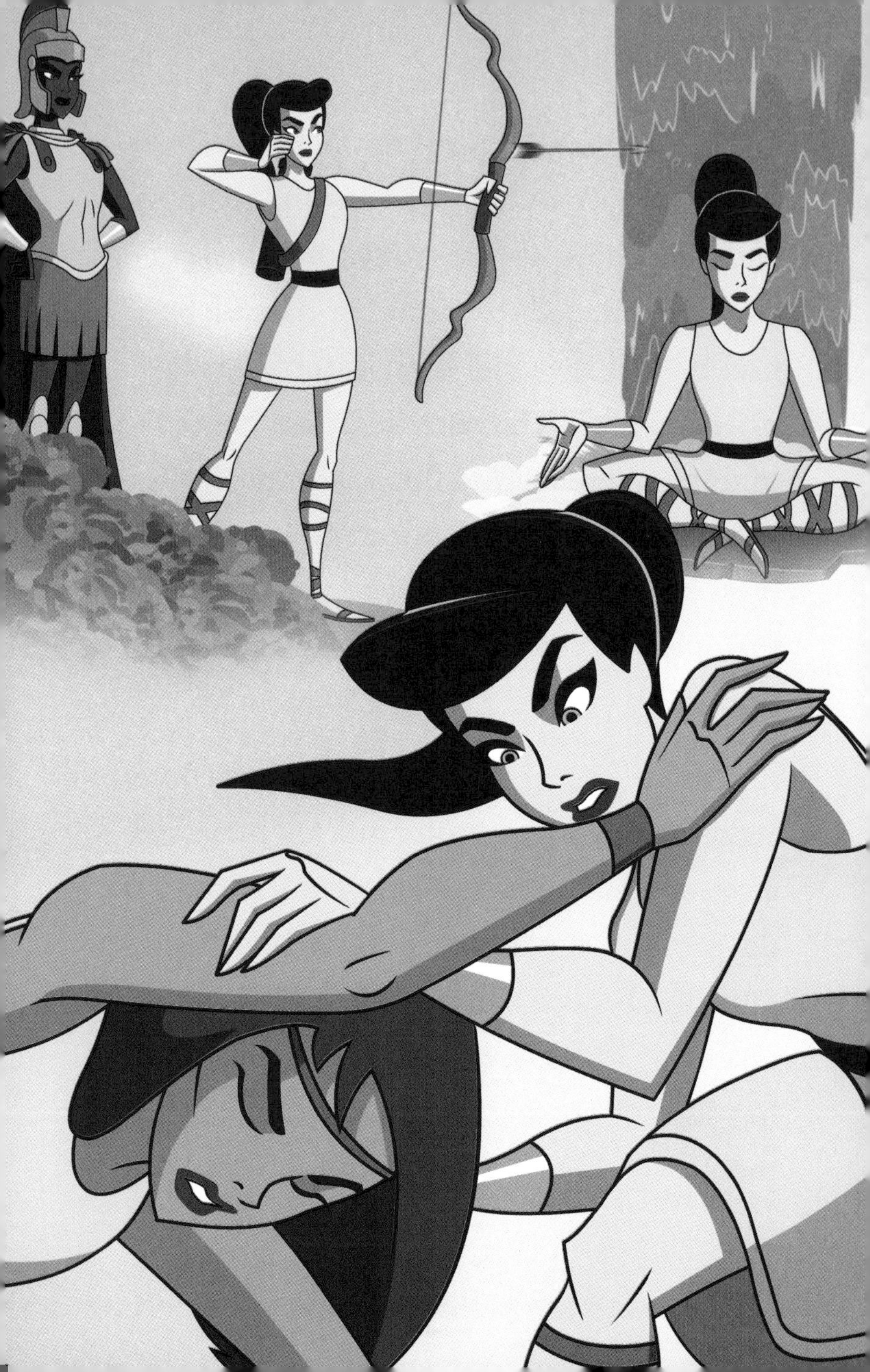

All of the Amazons praised the young princess's speed and strength. She was a true wonder. Despite her youth, she could beat the strongest warriors on the island. When Diana could easily defeat twenty warriors in one day, she felt her training must nearly be done. She approached the general, expecting great praise.

"You need to learn control," Phillipus growled. "You must match your foe step for step. Domination does not equal victory."

The words were harsh, but they made Diana work harder. At first, she didn't understand what Phillipus meant. She could defeat any opponent. Why should she change her tactics to match theirs? Then, slowly, Diana realized that the general had been right. When the goal is peace, there is no point in domination.

Soon, Wonder Woman began to win battles even more easily than before. She fought against opponent after opponent as she learned to control her powers.

Along with her mastery, Diana gained a new confidence. Now she was certain she was the strongest, fastest, and most able warrior on the island.

Phillipus saw that Diana had learned control, but also saw a new weakness emerging. The young princess's confidence would be her downfall.

She had one more lesson to learn.

# GROWING PAINS

Queen Hippolyta paced the floor nervously. She could not believe what Phillipus was asking her! Hippolyta had always trusted her general completely. When she had come to her asking to train the princess, it had been a hard request to grant. But the general had been right.

Phillipus's most recent request was even more difficult to grant. The queen could not bring herself to agree.

"One day it could save your daughter's life," Phillipus warned.

The general stood with her arms crossed. When she spoke, she looked into the queen's eyes. She did not waste words.

Hippolyta looked away. Once again she knew the general was right. Though she could not speak, she nodded her approval. The general turned and left silently.

The next morning, Diana woke with the sun. She began her day as she always did, by thanking the gods for their gifts. She dressed, ate, and then hurried outside to meet the general. Spring was in the air, and she was anxious to be done with work. Training had become a bore. There was no challenge in it. She always won effortlessly.

"Good morning, Princess," Phillipus called. The general, who was almost always clad in battle armor, was dressed in plain clothes on this day.

"Good morning," Diana replied. She waited for her teacher to explain.

"Today we are going on a hike," Phillipus announced.

Diana's heart leaped. It had been a long time since she had visited the animals in the forest. Quickly she began to remove her battle gear. The general watched her toss her sword and bow aside.

"Are you certain you won't need those?" the general asked. "A warrior must be prepared at all times."

Diana almost laughed out loud. The general had to be joking. Why would she need weapons in the forest? There would be no sparring partners to fight there. Besides, she could win any battle using only her bare hands.

Phillipus remained silent as the two set out. When they reached the base of the mountain, Diana climbed the steep trail happily. She was sure-footed on the rocky path, and hurried ahead of her teacher.

The sun was high when the princess finally spotted the small herd of deer. She called to them. The deer turned their ears in her direction. Before they could spring over to greet her, their ears twitched back. They'd heard something else.

Diana listened carefully, and she heard it, too. RUMMMMMMMBLE!

It sounded almost like thunder. It was coming from the ridge above them. Diana turned to look. She spotted an enormous boulder. It was rolling down the mountain and was headed right toward the herd of deer!

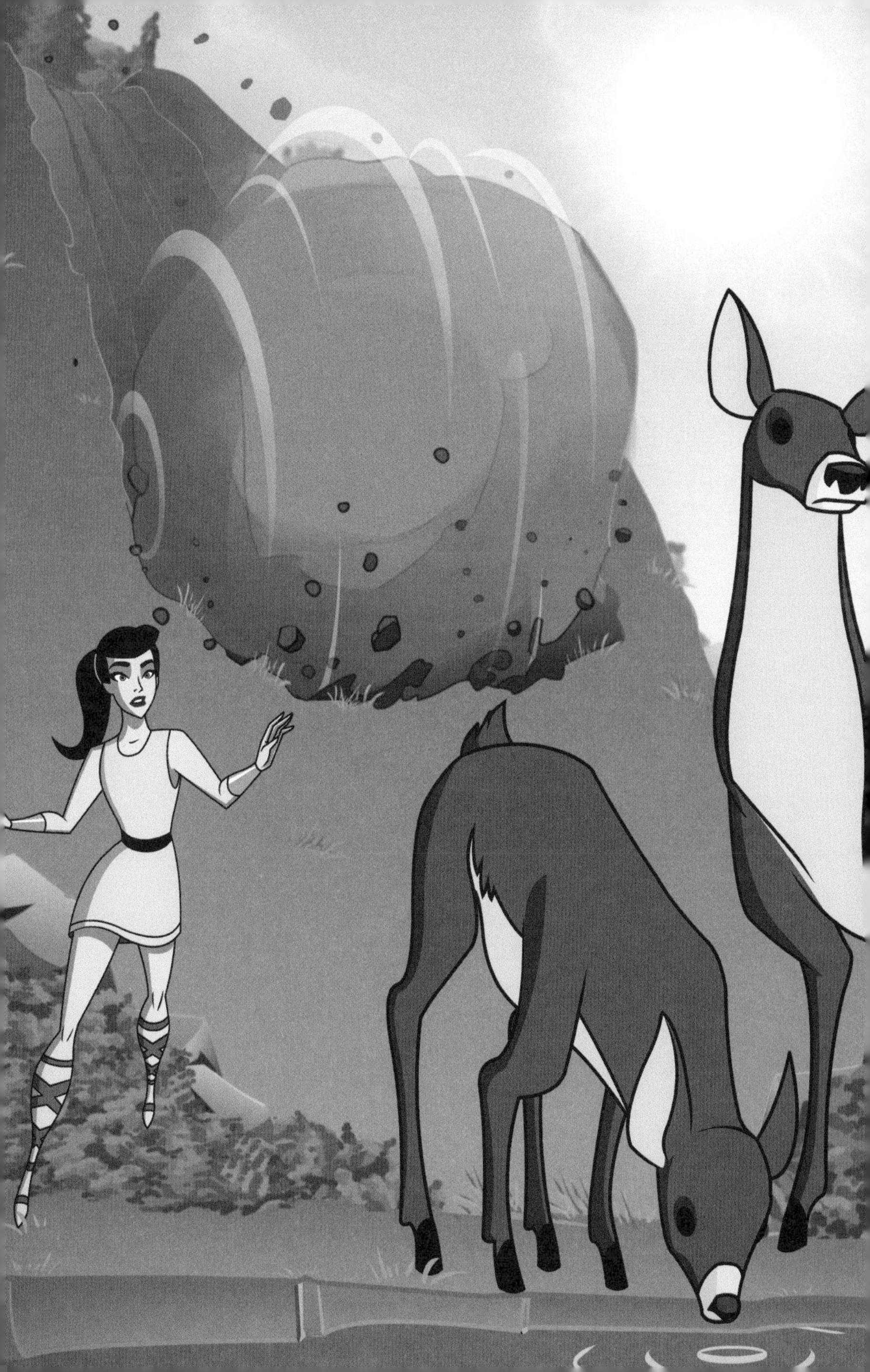

The huge rock was gathering speed. It was nearly three times larger than the young princess, but Diana did not flinch. She placed herself between the deer and the boulder. She braced herself with her back leg. The deer froze where they were. Smaller rocks began to shower them, bouncing ahead of the massive rock that was still tumbling down.

**BOOM!** The forest shook as the stone crashed into young Diana's waiting arms. A cloud of dust rose, and Diana slid backward several feet. Then, as the air cleared, Diana found her footing. Slowly she began to roll the rock up and away.

The birds called out, amazed at Diana's ability. The deer thanked her too. Diana felt proud and pushed faster. She could do anything! She could save anyone!

Her feeling of pride was so great that the girl didn't notice the stirrings in the woods around her. She did not realize she was about to be ambushed.

Princess Diana stood with her arms high. She held back the giant rock as hooded figures emerged from the trees. Suddenly, bows and arrows were aimed at her from all directions. She was surrounded!

Still unaware, Diana continued until one of the taller figures took aim with a rock sling. The attacker swung the sling over her head and fired. The rock found its target — Diana's braced leg. 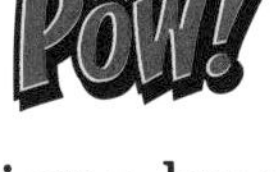
POW!

The pain took Diana by surprise. It was a new sensation to her. So was the feeling of fear she felt when she looked up to see she was outnumbered. If she released the rock, it would crush the animals in its path.

She could not fight and save her friends. The combination of pain and fear were nearly crippling to her.

Then, slowly, the rock-slinger lowered her hood, and Diana stared in disbelief. It was General Phillipus. Others also stepped forward, each one a member of the Amazon army.

The princess felt both relieved and ashamed. Her confidence had gotten the better of her. If the ambush had been real, it might have cost her friends their lives, as well as hers.

Princess Diana bowed her head, humbled. She had learned her lesson.

Although Diana did not notice, Phillipus smiled approvingly.

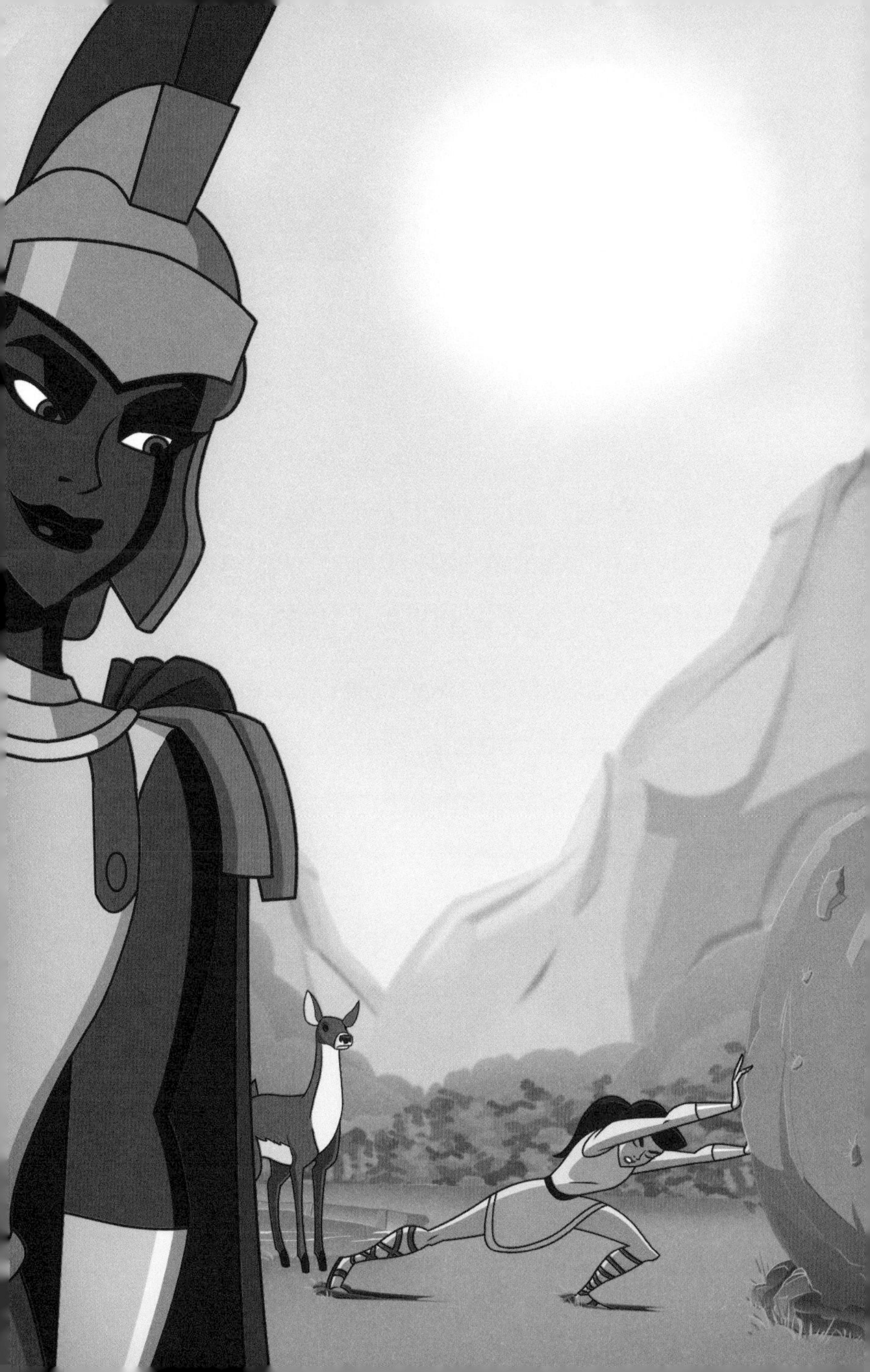

# CHAPTER 5

# LOST LESSONS

The pain in her leg woke Wonder Woman. She slowly opened her eyes.

Deva was still standing at the edge of the crater in the street. The evil girl waved her weapon. She was gloating and savoring her moment of victory.

Anyone watching would have thought that Devastation had the upper hand, and that the end was near for Wonder Woman. Deva was armed. She had an army of angry citizens ready to do whatever she asked.

She had Wonder Woman right where she wanted her, too — lying helpless at the bottom of a pit. But Wonder Woman knew the fight was not over. Her body was motionless, but the gears in her mind were turning rapidly.

"Look at you!" Deva said. "You've never looked better!" Wonder Woman's weakness delighted Deva, as did the small fights that were breaking out in the crowd. "Soon the whole world will be at war!" she screamed, watching the restless mob.

The Amazon Princess cringed. Deva's dream was Wonder Woman's nightmare. Yet it was the ways they were the same, and not their differences, that Wonder Woman found herself thinking about. Formed from the same clay, the two shared more than Deva had ever realized.

They both had otherworldly powers, near invincibility, and the confidence that came with being powerful.

General Phillipus's old lessons were fresh in Wonder Woman's mind. She saw clearly that Deva's pride was making her careless. The girl was so busy celebrating that she didn't notice when Wonder Woman freed her hands from under her body.

Yes, Wonder Woman and Deva shared many things, but not everything. The evil child cared for no one, while Wonder Woman felt for everyone — including her enemies. Even struggling for life, Wonder Woman felt compassion for Devastation. The poor thing had no idea what was about to happen.

With her eyes barely open, Wonder Woman tracked Deva's every move.

She watched Deva point her sword at her and stare down in disgust.

"Bye-bye, Princess," said Deva. "Wish I could say it's been wonderful, but it hasn't." She fired a bolt from her sword. The blast was aimed right at Wonder Woman's head!

With faster-than-lightning reflexes, Wonder Woman rolled to her back. She brought her silver cuffs in front of her face. In an instant, the bolt intended to kill her was deflected back at Deva.

**ZZZRRRRRTTT!** Deva was blasted by her own charge. If she had been alert, Deva might have noticed that Wonder Woman was awake. She might have been able to save herself.

With no time to lose, Wonder Woman got to her feet. She leaped from the crater.

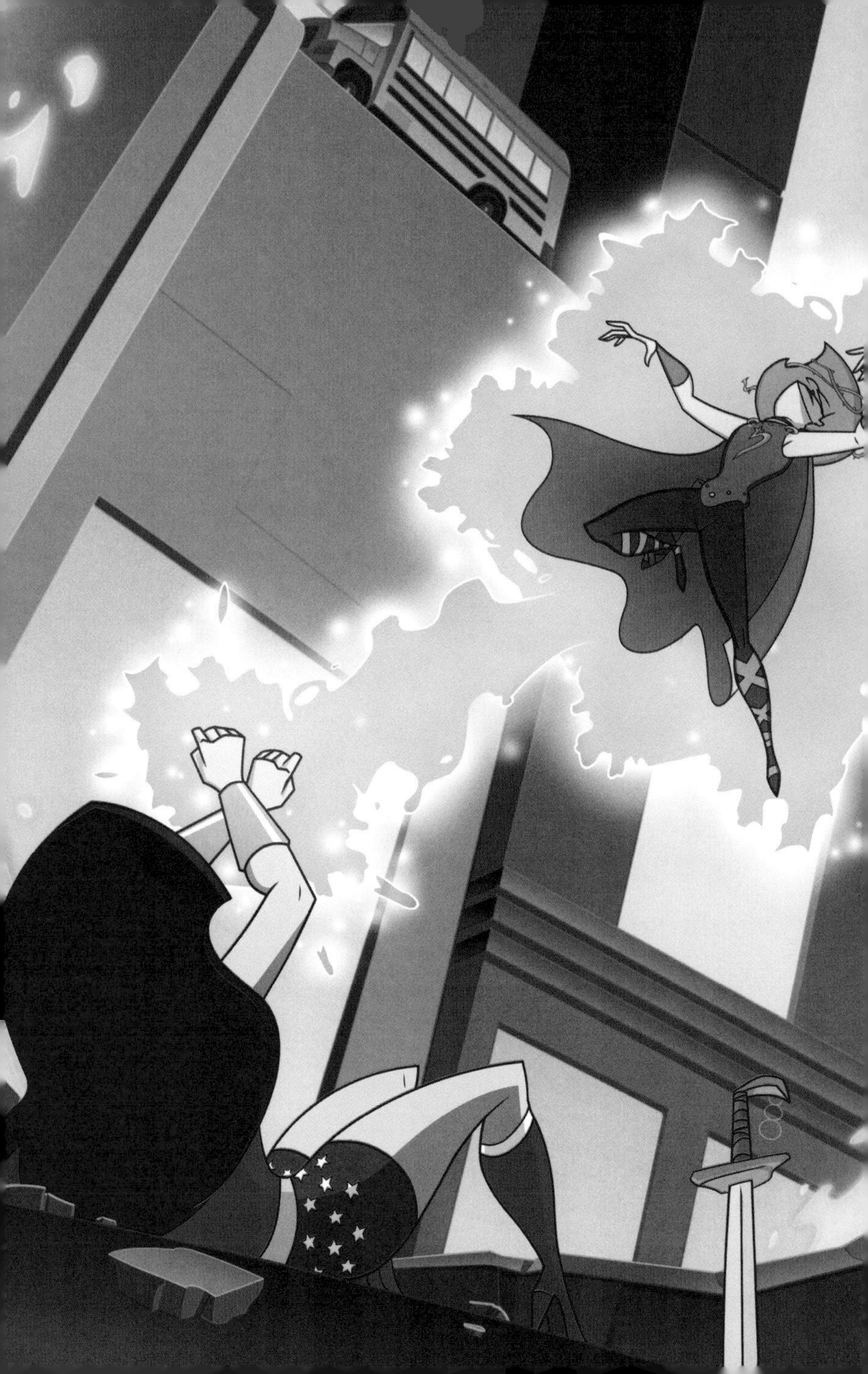

Wonder Woman stood ready to finish the fight. Nearby, she could hear the cheers of the people on the bus she had rescued. But there was no time for glory. Wonder Woman's mission was peace. To achieve it, there were still a few things she needed to take care of.

Deva reeled on the ground. Her weapon lay a short distance away. Wonder Woman picked up the sword and snapped it in two. **KRAK!** Then she kneeled down and tied up Deva with her Lasso of Truth.

A moment later, Deva was crying like a child. Wonder Woman was not sure if it was because her plan had failed, or because she felt a tiny bit of regret for what she had done.

With Deva's defeat, the anger in the streets faded away.

People began helping each other to their feet. They shook hands. They apologized to one another. They even began to clean up the mess they had made.

Deva sobbed. Wonder Woman looked at her, unsmiling, and thought of her teacher. "I think there may be hope for you yet," she told Deva.

"I don't want hope," Deva hissed back. She spat on the street.

"I know," Wonder Woman said. She looked down at Deva the way a disappointed mother might.

Together Wonder Woman and Devastation watched the citizens on Main Street restore the peace.

It would not be long before the city was a happy place once again.

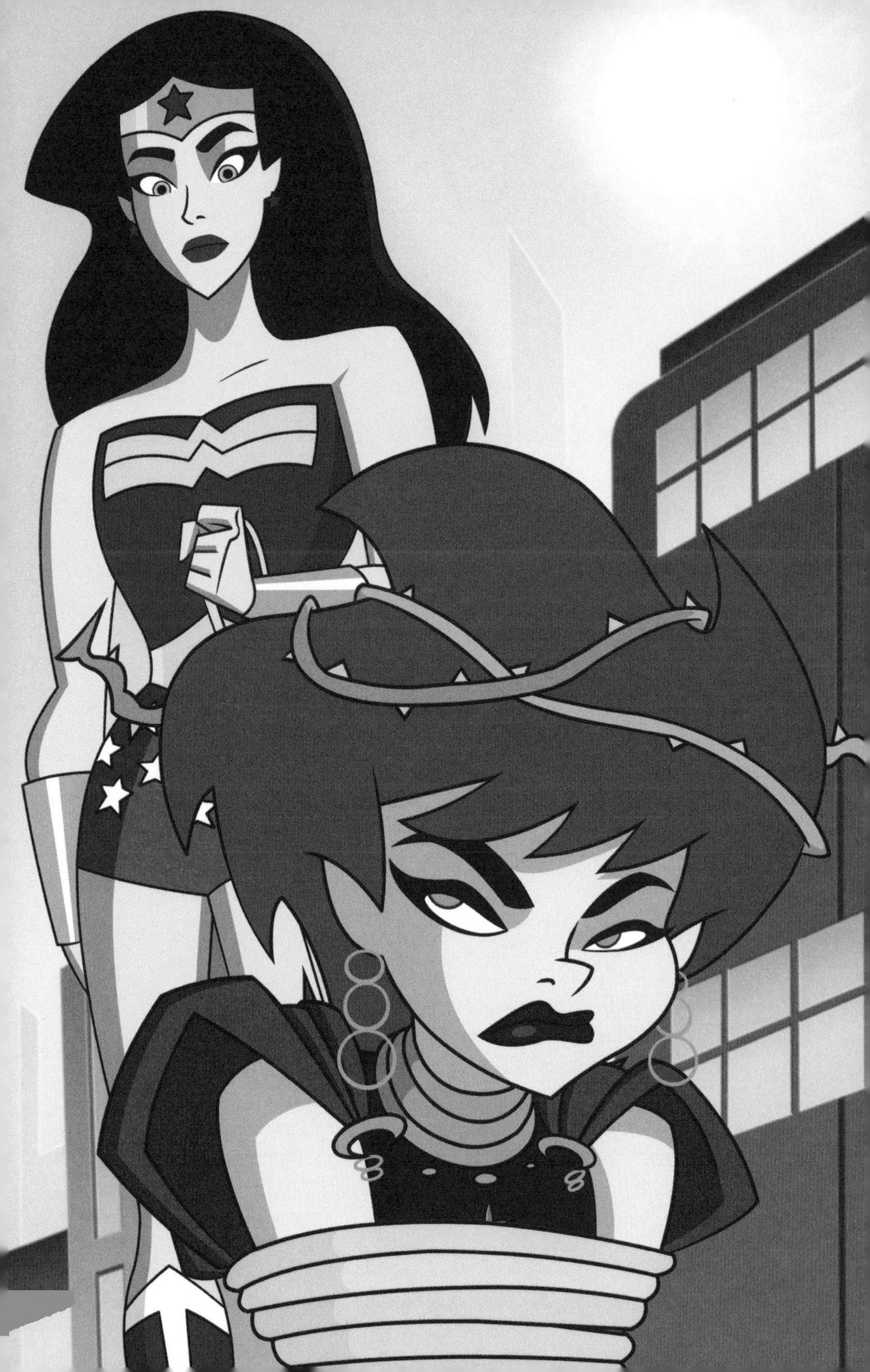

# INVISIBLE PLANE
## SECRET FILES

FILE NO. 3765 >>>DEVA

**ENEMY ››** ALLY FRIEND

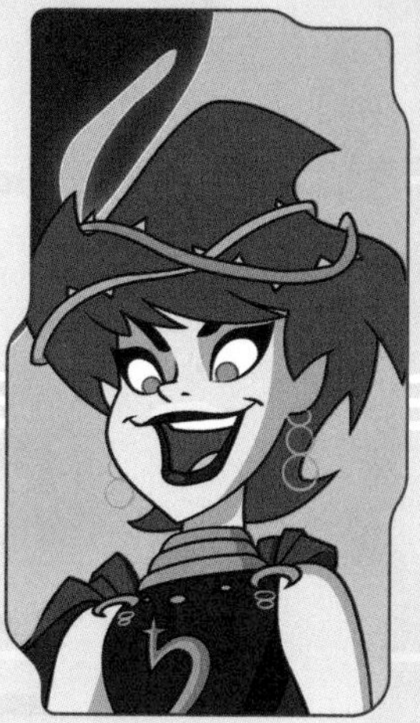

**REAL NAME:** Devastation

**BIRTHPLACE:** Themyscira

**HEIGHT:** 4 ft 2 in **WEIGHT:** 88 lbs

**EYES:** Blue **HAIR:** Red

**POWERS/ABILITIES:** Superhuman strength, super-speed, and flight. Expert in hand-to-hand combat. Can cause earthquakes at will and control other people's minds.

## BIOGRAPHY

Cronus, evil king of the Titans, was having a difficult time fighting off the incredible Wonder Woman. His solution: unleash Devastation upon the world. Cronus dripped a few drops of Wonder Woman's blood on the clay of Themyscira. Then, he shaped the clay into the figure of a young teen. Just like that, he had created an evil clone of Wonder Woman. Cronus named her Deva, short for Devastation, and asked each member of his army of gods to give her superpowers. Each amazing ability was given a dark twist to match Deva's sinister personality.

## POWERS

### GIFTS FROM THE GODS

HARRIER gave Deva the gift of super-speed and flight.

DISDAIN made her beautiful, and showed her how to control humans.

TITAN granted Deva super-strength and the ability to create earthquakes.

SLAUGHTER showed her how to kill any living thing.

ARCH made Deva's mind sharp.

OBLIVION showed her how to enter anyone's mind and shape their memories at will.

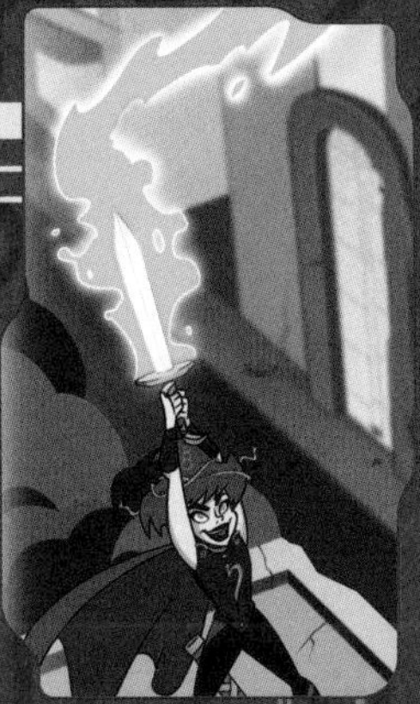

## WEAPON

### STAVING OFF DEVASTATION

Wonder Woman's Lasso of Truth can not only snare Deva, but it can also force her to hear and speak only the truth while she is wrapped in its golden coils. The lasso can stretch to infinite length, and is also unbreakable, ensuring that Deva couldn't break free once she was entangled. In the hands of Wonder Woman, the lasso is the perfect offense, and defense, against the destructive Deva.

# BIOGRAPHIES

**Sarah Hines Stephens** has authored more than 60 books for children, and written about all kinds of characters, from Jedi to princesses. Though she has some stellar red boots, she is still holding out for an invisible plane and thinks a Lasso of Truth could come in handy parenting her two wonder kids. When she is not writing, gardening, or saving the world by teaching about recycling, Sarah enjoys spending time with her heroic husband and super friends.

**Dan Schoening** was born in Victoria, B.C. Canada. From an early age, Dan has had a passion for animation and comic books. Currently, Dan does freelance work in the animation and game industry and spends a lot of time with his lovely little daughter, Paige.

# GLOSSARY

**abrupt** (uh-BRUPT)—sudden and unexpected

**ambushed** (AM-bushd)—attacked someone from a hiding place

**bouquet** (boh-KAY)—a bunch of picked or cut flowers

**compassion** (kuhm-PASH-uhn)—a feeling or desire to help someone who is in need

**culprit** (KUHL-prit)—a person who is guilty of doing something wrong or of committing a crime

**domination** (dom-uh-NAY-shun)—control or rule over someone or something

**enchanted** (en-CHAN-tid)—a place or thing that is enchanted has been put under a spell, or it seems magical

**sparring** (SPAHR-ing)—practicing boxing moves

**tactics** (TAK-tikz)—plans or methods

# DISCUSSION QUESTIONS

1. Deva was created to be evil. Do you think people are born bad, or do they become evil as they grow up? Explain.

2. Which of Wonder Woman's abilities or magical items helped her the most in this book? Why?

# WRITING PROMPTS

1. Deva is capable of manipulating the memories of others however she likes. Why would this be a dangerous skill to have? How could it be used to harm — or help — others? Write about it.

2. Why do you think Phillipus was so hard on Princess Diana? Was it fair that Phillipus tricked the young Amazon to teach her a lesson?

3. Wonder Woman had to push through a lot of pain to save the people of Washington, D.C. Have you ever had to deal with pain? Write about your painful experience.

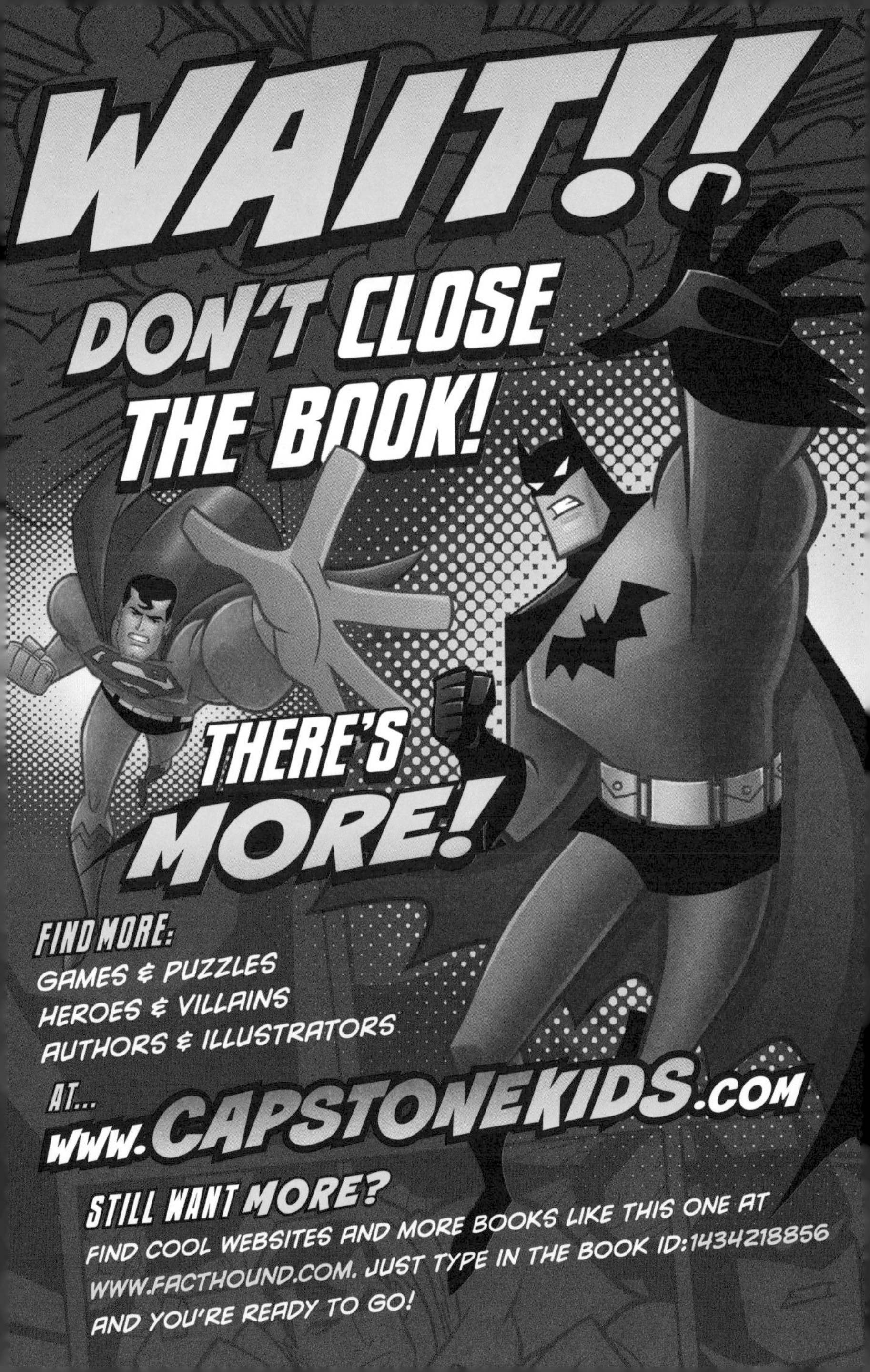
WAIT!!
DON'T CLOSE THE BOOK!
THERE'S MORE!
FIND MORE:
GAMES & PUZZLES
HEROES & VILLAINS
AUTHORS & ILLUSTRATORS
AT...
WWW.CAPSTONEKIDS.COM
STILL WANT MORE?
FIND COOL WEBSITES AND MORE BOOKS LIKE THIS ONE AT WWW.FACTHOUND.COM. JUST TYPE IN THE BOOK ID:1434218856 AND YOU'RE READY TO GO!

# MORE NEW WONDER WOMAN ADVENTURES!

DC COMICS™ SUPER HEROES
WONDER WOMAN
SIMONSON
SCHOENING
MONSTER MAGIC

MONSTER MAGIC

DC COMICS™ SUPER HEROES
WONDER WOMAN
TRIAL OF THE AMAZONS
DAHL • SCHOENING

TRIAL OF THE AMAZONS

DC COMICS™ SUPER HEROES
WONDER WOMAN
ATTACK OF THE CHEETAH
MASON
SCHOENING

ATTACK OF THE CHEETAH

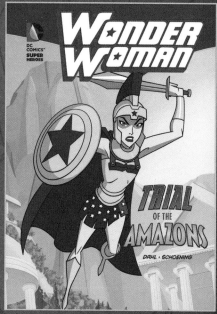